ALWAYS FAITHFUL

ALWAYS FAITHFUL

PATRICK JONES

darbycreek
MINNEAPOLIS

The author wishes to thank Susan Olson, Professional Counselor, M.Ed., LPC, for her expertise on military families and thoughtful review of manuscripts in the Support and Defend series, and Judith Klein for her proofreading and copyediting wizardry.

Darby Creek
A division of Lerner Publishing Group, Inc.
241 First Avenue North
Minneapolis, MN 55401 USA

For reading levels and more information, look up this title at www.lernerbooks.com.

The images in this book are used with the permission of: © Rubberball/Getty Images (teen girl); © iStockphoto.com/CollinsChin (background); © iStockphoto.com/mart_m (dog tags).

Main body text set in Janson Text LT Std 12/17.5.
Typeface provided by Adobe Systems.

Library of Congress Cataloging-in-Publication Data

The Cataloging-in-Publication Data for *Always Faithful* is on file at the Library of Congress.
ISBN 978-1-4677-8052-0 (lib. bdg.)
ISBN 978-1-4677-8093-3 (pbk.)
ISBN 978-1-4677-8820-5 (EB pdf)

Manufactured in the United States of America
1 – SB – 7/15/15

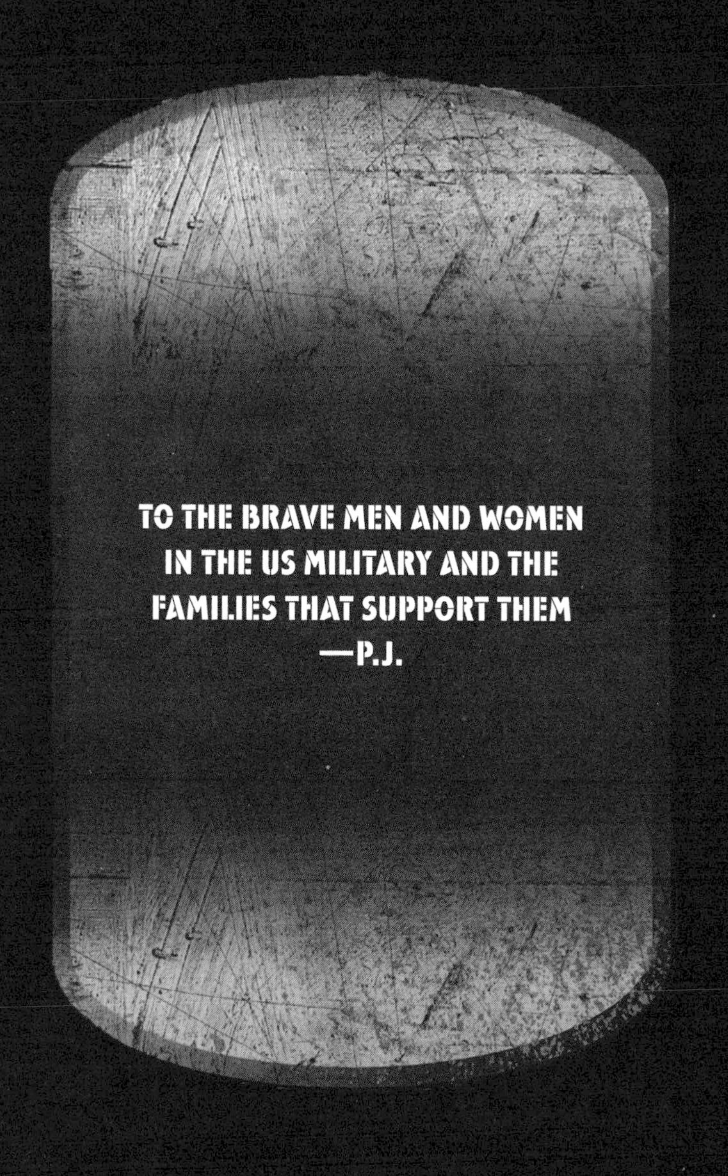

TO THE BRAVE MEN AND WOMEN
IN THE US MILITARY AND THE
FAMILIES THAT SUPPORT THEM
—P.J.

0

MAY 10 / SUNDAY MORNING
MOTHER'S DAY

"Double time, girls!" my dad yells. It's Staff Sgt. Ray Alvirde's only volume. Twelve years in the Marine Corps, the last three as a Staff Sergeant, will lead to that sort of thing. It's an occupational hazard but hardly the worst for a Marine. Being shot or blown up by an IED are much higher on the list.

"I hate that expression," I whisper to my younger sister Lucinda, who's in middle school.

With Dad it's always got to be "double time"—he couldn't just ask us to hurry up.

"More like double chin," Lucinda jokes. I stifle a laugh. My dad left the Marines two years ago. Since then, he's gained twenty pounds, held and lost ten jobs, and loses his temper ten times a day with me and with Lucinda but never with Chavo, our younger brother. *Mi niño de oro.*

"Get the lead out," Dad yells. A strange expression for a man shot in combat three times. With the bullet fragments in his body, he'd never make it through an airport metal detector, not that we ever go anyplace. We live in San Diego, CA, as close to paradise as possible. But it's more that Dad said he's never getting on a plane again. Except when he says it, the word "plane" is surrounded by four letter words in proportion to the number of Tecates gone from the six-pack.

It's Mother's Day and we're supposed to cook Mom breakfast in bed. Dad's orders. Then to church—Mom's orders. Then to a big family picnic: lots of food, beer, laughing. I know for sure about the first two, but I can only hope on the last one since Dad doesn't laugh much anymore, except when he stays up late drinking with Victor.

Lucinda crawls out of bed first. We've shared a room going on a year. She moved in with me when Victor, Dad's down-on-his-luck Marine buddy, took her room.

"Only a few weeks, Lucy," always truthful, always faithful Dad said forty weeks ago. Like Dad, Victor's struggling to make it back into civilian life. He mostly drinks; Dad yells. I think I like Victor's way much better.

"So is Miguel coming?" Lucinda asks. Miguel is my boyfriend of four months and fourteen days. We were each other's New Year's resolution. "If so, who will I talk to?"

"You can keep Victor company," I say. "Or at least count his cervezas for him."

"Rosie, do you ever have anything to say that's not a smart mouth answer?"

"No," I say, rolling over and pulling the covers up.

She cracks up. The laughter irritates Dad, who must be outside our door like he's keeping watch. He pounds on the door so hard it feels like a Southern California quake starting.

"Double time," he shouts for the second time. The seriousness of his voice cracks us both up. I picture him outside the door, steaming mad like some cartoon bull ready to charge.

"We'll hurry up," I say. He walks away, although it sounds more like marching.

"Even with all of that—" Lucinda points at the door and mimics Dad's stiff manner. She waves her hand over her head, mocking his crew cut, and pulls her pants out, mocking his beer belly. "Even with all that going on, I'm glad he's home. I thought he'd never make it."

"I think there's only one person who wishes Dad was still deployed," I say softly.

Lucinda yanks a shirt on. "Who?"

I point toward the door. "Staff Sgt. Ray Alvirde."

2

MAY 12 / TUESDAY MORNING

"What did you get?" I ask Miguel. There's a big smile on his pretty face, so I'm guessing my A-student, National Honor Society, volunteer tutor boyfriend did just fine, as always.

"Better than Alejandro," he whispers.

I'm confused. Alejandro is Miguel's gang-banger older brother. "What did he get?"

"Someday it will be five to ten, pending appeal."

"And what are you going to get?" I ask, knowing the answer, setting him up.

"A commission to the Corps." Miguel thinks his role as an ROTC captain will help him.

"Rosie, Miguel, I need your attention," Mr. Richards says. He's this old white guy with thick glasses, ugly clothes, and a bit of a lisp. And I want to be just like him. I always did well in school—Dad wouldn't have it any other way—but I never cared about it until this year, taking chemistry with Richards. I'll have Richards again next year for biology.

"Yes, sir!" Miguel says.

Richards laughs. "You're not in the Corps yet, Miguel, so take it down a notch."

Miguel doesn't laugh—he's perfect, other than lacking a sense of humor—but I do.

"So, Rosie, did you sign up for those summer enrichment courses at UCSD?" Richards asks me.

"The second you told me about them."

He sips from his ever-present coffee cup. "That will give you a head start with science, and you'll sign up for AP Bio next year?"

I sit up straight. My long black hair touches my chair. "No, because you're not teaching it."

"That's the problem with all of you Marine kids," he says. He smiles, but I sense a seriousness in his voice. "You're too used to following orders. Think for yourself."

I stand up and salute him, which makes him laugh. "If you say so, sir!"

Mr. Richards snorts coffee through his nose, an unplanned science experiment gone wrong.

3

MAY 15 / FRIDAY NIGHT

"Paydays are the worst," I tell Lucinda, speaking loud to be heard over our parents arguing below our room.

"I wish I had a boyfriend so I had someplace to go," she says. We're in our room. I'm getting ready for my date with Miguel. "Doesn't Miguel have a younger brother?"

"No, just an older one and he's bad news," I answer. "Maybe you and Chavo could . . ."

"He's at some soccer deal," she reminds me.

"They'll go watch him, of course."

"If they don't kill each other first!" I joke, but it's not funny. My parents fight a lot. Well, Dad mostly yells, but I've never seen a bruise or heard a punch thrown. The fighting never happened much until Dad came home two years ago, when he resigned from the Marines under pressure from Mom, I think. I don't know; I stay out of their lives and wish they'd give me the same courtesy.

"It's Victor's fault," she says. Angry that he took over her room, Lucinda blames him for everything.

I don't say anything. Mostly we all feel sorry for Victor, but it does seem like he's dragging my dad down with him. Both spend most of their days when they're not working—now at Home Depot—cursing the VA, remembering their fallen brothers, and reliving missions.

"I have to go." I glance in the mirror: big brown hair, little red dress. I don't need an A in science to know Miguel likes those elements combined. He'll like my white prom dress tomorrow, too.

I gather my things and head down the stairs, not sneaking out but not calling attention.

"Once you've worn the uniform, you can't wear another!" Dad shouts. He follows with a string of profanity, mostly in Spanish. Curse words are the only Spanish he speaks at home these days.

"Raymond, give it time," Mom pleads.

My hand is on the knob and I should leave, but—

"Then you wear it!" There's an odd sound, then an ugly orange Home Depot polo shirt sails from the living room into the kitchen, landing at my feet. "I quit that stupid job."

It's better he quit than get fired again, like the last job, the one before that, and the one . . .

4

MAY 17 / SUNDAY EARLY MORNING

"Thank you sir, may I have another?" I coo at Miguel after a particularly delicious kiss. We're on my front porch after prom. The night went better than expected, considering how high expectations are for a lousy dinner and bad music. I brush my hand against his clean-shaven face.

"With pleasure." He looks fine in his Marine blue ROTC dress uniform rather than a tux.

He holds me tight. I press against him.

Miguel's about to say something, but Tino—his drop-out older cousin who drove us with his date—honks the horn. "I gotta go," Miguel whispers. We were hoping there might be an opportunity for more, but my stupid curfew and Tino are conspiring against us.

One last kiss, then he's back to Tino's rust-bucket ride, our prom night chariot. I watch the taillights disappear into the darkness, wishing I could remember this moment forever, until—

"You're late, Rosalita Maria!" Dad says, charging out the front door. When the middle name drops, I usually run for cover.

I look at my phone. He's right, I'm wrong, I'll own it. "I'm sorry, but I'm only an hour late."

He thrusts his right arm at me, the one with the Rolex knockoff on his wrist and Semper Fi tattoo on the forearm. "In-country, if you're one second late for a mission, somebody dies."

Mom's in the background. Silent.

"I said I'm sorry, but nobody's going to die because—"

"It's about keeping your word!" His forearm's right in front of my face. He jabs at the tattoo with his left index finger, over and over. "Always faithful! You will not fail!"

I start to say something, but then I stop because he's not listening. He sighs deeply, like I punched him or something, and stalks toward the kitchen—probably to kill another Tecate, not the Taliban. Although maybe that's not true because lately he's drinking less and spending time working out with Victor since they don't have a job to go to any more.

Mom comes toward me. She reaches out, but I'm not interested in her too-little, too-late.

"Rosie, forgive him." Her voice is hoarse. "It's a hard time right now for your father."

"What does he mean, you will not fail in your mission?"

She answers with silence.

"I'm his daughter, not his soldier," I say as I walk slowly, almost wounded, up the stairs.

5

MAY 19 / TUESDAY MORNING

"Rosalita, please sit down," my school counselor Mr. Torrez says. "I know you're studying for finals, so thanks for meeting with me. I want to talk about your senior schedule."

"Sure," I say and smile. He frowns, then starts talking really fast about all my choices.

"I understand you're not taking the AP biology course? You certainly qualify."

"I'm not taking AP Bio because I want to take science with Mr. Richards, and—"

He cuts me off. "AP Bio would be perfect for college, then medical school."

"I don't want to be a doctor," I remind him. We've had this conversation before.

"Do you plan to join the Corps like your father?" That's another of his favorites.

"I want to be a science teacher like Mr. Richards."

He frowns again, like his dog died, and he starts asking about other courses. This time, my answer's not as noble.

"Well, my boyfriend Miguel is . . ." I start.

"That's not a good reason, Rosalita, because by fall he may not be your boyfriend."

I'd like to make him frown with a kick in the balls. "I'm sticking with these courses."

"You have the tenacity of a Marine." He points at the walls of his office. He's got the Marine flag, photos, ribbons, all of it. It's like the corner of my dad's room: a Marine museum.

"What is it with you guys?" I ask him, since it's not something I can discuss with Dad.

"The Corps is a calling." Like Dad, he's got to show me his Semper Fi tattoo. I swear Marines flash their tattoos more often and with more pride than any gang-banger in San Diego. "How is your dad readjusting to civilian life? For some, it's hard, but there are resources . . ."

"He does all of that," I say. "I thought he'd be home more, but it's like he's still in the Corps. He's always attending meetings at the VA, helping Victor and other vets out."

"You can leave the Corps," Mr. Torrez says. "But it never leaves you."

6

MAY 25 / MONDAY
MEMORIAL DAY / LATE MORNING

"He's crying," I whisper to Lucinda as I point at Chavo. "Dad won't like that."

Lucinda stifles a laugh, which is smart given the circumstances and surroundings.

The whole family, along with lots of Dad's Corps buddies and a couple thousand Corps-connected people are under a hot sun at Fort Rosecrans National Cemetery. We're at the opening ceremony for the Memorial Day celebration, the biggest in California, Dad brags.

I'm not sure why Chavo is crying as they read the list of the fallen from the past year. I recall when I was little, when both of the wars were still raging, the lists seemed to go on forever. Now, it's a few names, but there's no chance one will be Staff Sgt. Ray Alvirde.

"He'd better man up," Lucinda whispers, something Dad is always saying to Chavo.

Like double time, I hate that expression, but I let it go. It's not the time or place to argue with my sister or even mock my little brother. My parents keep generating enough turmoil for a family of fifteen, let alone five. But this morning, they stand united. I put my hand over my eyes to block the sun. Last year it rained, but we stood out here anyway. When Dad was deployed, Mom didn't make us come, but if he was home, we went. No discussion allowed.

"We are gathered today," the Fort Pendleton chaplain starts. Every time I hear him speak, I feel sick to my stomach. I recall the nights I'd laid in bed, imagining what words he'd say at my father's funeral, which I expected to attend before I went to my first prom.

I see Chavo's got it together, standing proud if not tall. Dad, who is no giant, towers over Chavo and Mom like an old oak, especially this morning. Standing tall and straight, looking healthier than he has in a year, wearing his dark blue dress uniform with gold buttons and colorful ribbons, Dad looks like a totally different man than a few weeks ago when he was just a short, fat guy working at the Home Depot. I stare into Dad's eyes. I see pride and purpose. And it makes me afraid. Very afraid.

7

MAY 26 / TUESDAY EARLY EVENING

"You don't have to worry," Dad says, like that makes a difference. He dropped a bomb and we're expected not to appear wounded. After he passes the physical, he's re-enlisting in the Marines effective July 1.

"I thought you were home for good!" Lucinda whines.

Dad's all blank stares. He hands us each a copy of the Basic Re-enlistment Prerequisites. "I meet them all," he says. "This is what's best for me, for all of us. Isn't that right, Jaclyn?"

Mom nods slowly, more like a recruit following an order than a partner in a marriage.

"Now, Chavo, you'll be the man of the house while I'm gone. *¡Hombre de la casa!*"

"Rosie?" he says. This is my second worst nightmare come true. Dad being dead is the first; his rejoining is second because it leads right back to the first.

"Rosie, your father is talking to you," Mom says. She sounds tired already. Maybe since we're all older and can take care of ourselves, she urged him to rejoin. I don't know. I don't care.

"This doesn't change anything," Dad says. "Well, except for you, Lucinda."

Lucinda stops crying long enough to listen—she's the only one crying because Chavo knows better. I suspect Mom shed her tears in private like always. And sadness isn't what I'm feeling at all.

"What are you talking about?" she asks.

"Victor is rejoining too, so you'll get your room back," he says. For some reason, being thrown this bone does nothing to stop her waterworks. "It will be okay."

Stone cold silent, I rise from the table and walk to the counter. I grab a box of tissues and a pair of scissors. I hand the tissues to Lucinda. I use the scissors to slice the Basic Re-enlistment Prerequisites sheet in half, quarters, eighths, shreds. Pieces fall to the floor like snowflakes. "Rosalita . . ." Dad starts, but he's drowned out when I slam the front door behind me, shattering the glass. The shards of glass join the pieces of paper and my siblings as shrapnel in the kitchen.

8

MAY 27 / WEDNESDAY MORNING

"Rosalita, wake up," Miguel whispers. "You're supposed to be studying."

I ignore him and let my face press against my open biology textbook.

"Miss Alvirde," Mr. Richards says. Like parents with the middle name, when a teacher drops the miss or mister bomb, it's not a good sign.

"Leave me alone," I hiss at Mr. Richards since I can't talk to Dad.

Dad was still up when I came home after an

hour of walking circles with no shoes in our neighborhood near the Camp Pendleton base. I didn't call Miguel or a friend. I couldn't hear Mr. ROTC Miguel say that he agreed with my dad. And since we'd started dating, I hadn't kept up with my friends. This was too heavy to restart a friendship with. I just walked in circles until my feet bled red into my white socks. When Dad tried to talk to me, I said, "*You're leaving me again.*"

"Miss Alvirde, you need to wake up or I'll send you to the office." Strict tone.

"No," I say. I put my head back on my book. He gives me another chance, but I just re-enlist sarcasm. "Actually, I'm conducting an experiment to see if osmosis really works."

Nobody laughs, not even Miguel. Typical. Richards calls Security to take me to the office since I have no intention of leaving this chair. When the security officer arrives, I stand up. The guy's wearing a uniform. I hate it. I hate uniforms. He says something smart and I lunge at him.

"Rosie, no!" Miguel jumps from his seat and grabs me before I hit Mr. Uniform.

The room explodes in noise. This scene—a student trying to hit Security or a teacher—is an everyday thing at my school, except that that student usually isn't honor roll member Rosalita Alvirde.

"I hope you can get yourself together, Miss Alvirde," Mr. Richards says, the sternness is gone and there's an actual thin reed of caring and concern. "Now, class, about your final."

Miguel's still holding onto me, whispering in my ear. "Chill, Rosie, chill."

"Can you help me, son?" the security officer asks Miguel.

Miguel nods. And in that nod, standing next to the guy in uniform, I see Miguel after two years at Parris Island. I hate him, too.

9

MAY 29 / FRIDAY MORNING

"Rosalita, I'm very disappointed in you," Mr. Torrez, King of the Obvious, says. After serving a one-day in-school suspension, I'm allowed back in class but only after a "check-in."

He's right, but I'm silent. Agreeing with any Marine, active or former, isn't on my list.

"I spoke with your father," he says, which is more than I've done. Dad is a black hole.

"So," is the two-letter word I say; FU are the two letters on the tip of my tongue.

"He told me of his decision to rejoin the Corps. He says you're upset." All hail the King!

"No."

"You seem like you're upset," he says to me, the girl wearing baggy unwashed clothes, no makeup, her hair a crow's nest, her arms across her chest, and biting her bottom lip raw.

"I'm not upset." King of the Obvious, please meet the Queen of Denial.

He reaches into his desk. "I know you attended support groups before," he natters on. "The Corps' outreach to families is top-notch, much stronger than when you were younger."

"So am I."

"What?"

"Stronger," I say. "So I don't need you or your support groups. I don't need anything."

Torrez rises from his desk. If he puts that tattooed Semper Fi arm on my shoulder, I'll bite it. "Rosie, the school is here for you. I'm here for you. The Corps is here for you. The . . ."

I cut him off. "But he's not. My dad, he's not

here for me, is he, Mr. Torrez? Is he?"

Torrez shakes his head. "Your dad's part of something bigger than a family. The Corps . . ."

I stand, kick the chair out behind me. "I don't need another list. Can I go to class?"

"Rosie, I want you to see someone about getting your anger under control."

I exit with a whisper stream of Spanish profanity. I slam the door; unfortunately, the glass holds.

10

MAY 29 / FRIDAY EVENING

"Rosie, come out of your room and talk to your father," Mom implores me. I check the door to make sure it's locked, which is against Dad's rules, but it's not like I care anymore.

"Unlock the door and at least talk with me. I'm worried about you."

"If you want to talk with someone, talk with Dad and tell him not to go away again."

"Rosie, it's too late." Her voice is hoarse again, from crying, not yelling, I assume. "He's already signed the papers. He's just got to—"

I slam my open palm against the door. "I don't care. You talked him into resigning. Why couldn't you talk him into staying home with us?" I wait for an answer, but none comes.

"Answer me!" Two more palm blows, but the pain and silence just grow deeper. "Fine."

"Rosalita, open this door!" The cavalry has arrived, or the Marine version of it. "I'm sorry, but I've made my decision. You're seventeen, almost an adult. I expect you to behave like one."

Dad said his vows to mom, to the Corps, and I make a vow, too. I refuse to speak to him.

"I didn't come to this decision lightly," he says and he starts explaining his reasons again, like somehow the tenth time he does it, I'll suddenly accept it.

"Rosie, listen . . ." Mom starts, but Dad tells her to be quiet. They're at it again in English and Spanish. I hear Mom threaten Dad: if he deploys again, she'll leave him, take us kids away.

"That worked once, Jaclyn. It won't work

again," he says. "Now, Rosie open this door!"

I check once more that it's locked. I pull Lucinda's bed in front of the door—she's at Grandma Rita's place—then pile other furniture on top. Dad alternates between pulling on the knob and pounding on the door. I gather a few things and open the bedroom window.

I throw my bag down on the grass and leap to the tall oak by the house. By the time he breaks through the barricade, I'll be gone. He's rejoining the Corps; I'm deserting my unit.

10

JUNE 1 / MONDAY MORNING

When I get to my locker, Miguel's waiting. I guess I knew I couldn't avoid him forever.

"I'm staying at Grandma Rita's for a while," I tell Miguel before he can say anything. I don't say I'm sleeping there because that's a lie: I can't sleep or eat. I can barely breathe.

"I'm worried about you, Rosie." He caresses my cheek. "What's wrong?"

Here goes. "My dad's re-enlisting in the Marines and he's—"

"I know. He told me. When you wouldn't return my calls or texts, I contacted your family," Miguel, the traitor, interrupts. "You should be proud of him, Rosie, serving his country—"

I push Miguel away. "I'm not proud of him! I'm so angry at him, I want to kill him!"

Miguel gets this odd look on his face, like he's embarrassed. We're fighting in public, but that happens all the time at this school. Except not to ROTC captains and honor rollers. The bell rings for class. Miguel puts his hand out, like I'm supposed to grab it, follow him. Obey.

"Come on, Rosie, we need to get to class. It's finals," he says. I don't move an inch. He stares at me, more hurt than angry; I stare at him in the opposite proportion. He checks his phone, sighs, and runs off toward class. I stand by my locker and wait for the second bell. It goes off, louder than I remember since I'm never in the hallway for it. Always on time Rosie.

I close my locker. Down the hallway, teachers close doors to give their finals. I grab my bag and walk slowly toward Mr. Richards' classroom. I keep walking until I get to the end of the hallway in the west wing. If Dad won't listen to my words, maybe he will listen to my actions.

When I open the exit door, the alarm screams. I cover my ears and race through the school parking lot. Once out on the street, I look for the closest bus stop. It's not that far.

"Do buses stop here any time soon?"

An older woman sitting on the bench nods and smiles at me. "Where are you going, honey?"

I pull change from my pocket. Count out a dollar fifty. "It depends which bus I get on."

12

JUNE 5 / FRIDAY MORNING

"You flunked all of your finals!" Dad shouts at me. I'm with him, Mom, and Mr. Torrez, which is way too many Marines in an office this small.

After I bailed on Monday, I knew I couldn't run away without getting into tons of trouble. Grandma Rita told Lucinda and me that we had to go home. With no place and no one else—Miguel and I are not talking and presumed broken up—I returned home, angry and silent.

"There has to be some mistake," Mom says.

"Rosie's always done so well in school."

I want to tell her there's no mistake. On the multiple-choice tests, I picked random answers as quickly as possible, then took the rest of the time napping at my desk. On the short answers, I wrote nothing that made any sense. On essay questions, I wrote even more nonsense.

"This means she'll need to attend summer school," Mr. Torrez says, like I'm not there. Now that I'm a failure, Mr. Marine Torrez won't speak my name. I'm just a "she" all of a sudden.

Finally I speak so they'll know I'm alive and kicking. "I'm not doing summer school."

"Then you'll repeat eleventh grade," Torrez fires back, machine gun fast.

"She will attend summer school. Mark my words," Dad says with a dagger stare at me.

"What if I don't?" I ask the three-judge panel. They look at me like I'm a space alien.

Dad's angry, Mom's hurt, and Mr. Torrez looks like he'd rather be anyplace but here, even Iraq. "Then you're a truant and could be arrested. Is that what you want, Rosie?" Mr. Torrez asks.

"If I go to juvie, then I'd get to wear a nice uniform like you two."

Mom starts to cry.

"Look what you've done to your mother!" Dad shouts.

"What I've done?" I start, and then maybe it's the small room, the idea of summer school, the Marine tag-team, but I finally let loose all my anger at Dad for rejoining.

He answers exactly how I would. He turns, exits, and slams the door. He's stronger than me, so this time, the glass breaks.

13

JUNE 10 / WEDNESDAY MORNING

"Rosie Alvirde?" A short black woman behind her desk calls my name.

"Here," I mumble. It's how everyone else answered, so I want to fit in. But as I glance around the room, I realize that's impossible. They're the kind of kids I've always avoided, but now I'm going to spend the summer with them. I don't think I'm better. I just want to avoid trouble, which most of them find—like Miguel's brother Alejandro and his cousin Tino.

"This is eleventh grade chemistry. My name is Mrs. Jackson," she starts and I'm bored already.

"Whatcha doing here?" A girl whispers from behind me. It's Brooke, Tino's ditzy prom date.

I don't respond because I don't like the answer. "Well, Brooke, I deliberately failed my finals because I was angry at my dad for rejoining the Marine Corps and leaving us. What? How did that hurt anyone but me? Well, funny thing about that, it didn't. So here I am."

"How's Tino?" I ask to change the subject. Jackson's still on a monotone roll.

"My boo's a'right."

I try not to roll my eyes at another white girl trying to sound black. "You still hooking up with Miguel?"

She assumes that since she's seventeen and having sex, I am too. "Maybe."

"I'd heard you was on the outs," says Brooke, who knows and talks too much. "We should get together—" Brooke starts but stops when Mrs. Jackson calls her out.

Brooke shuts up, but when Jackson starts talking about what we're going to learn—stuff I already know that Mr. Richards taught a hundred times better than this robo-teacher—I'd rather listen to Brooke. But mostly I want to talk to Miguel and see where we stand.

I ignore Jackson and glance around the room: battle scars, colors, and tattoos. It sounds like the start of an unfunny riddle: what's the difference between a Marine and a gang member? Answer: None. They're loyal to each other over all else, even their own flesh and blood.

14

JUNE 11 / THURSDAY EARLY EVENING

"We need to talk." Miguel's outside my front door. I left him no choice but to come over by refusing to return calls, texts, and chats. Deep down, I know I need him more than ever now, but I just don't know how to even explain what I'm feeling. And I'm afraid he won't understand.

"This won't take long." I block the door as best I can. He's got a hand behind his back. If it was Tino, I'd suspect a 9mm but instead Miguel pulls out a bouquet of a dozen flowers.

"I don't know what I said or what I did, but . . ." he starts. I open the door and I take the flowers, but I don't let him inside. I smell them, anything to avoid making eye contact. They can go on the grave of our relationship. Born in January, died in June. Cause of death, Rosie's father.

"I'm sorry," Miguel says, his voice as soft as his eyes. "I guess I should've known you were upset about your dad. I took his side. That was wrong. I'm sorry and I want you to know I—"

"You can leave." I stare at his shoes, beat up red All-Stars. In two years, they'll be boots shined so bright that the commandant at Parris Island will be able to see his face in them.

He reaches for me. I back away like he's a leper, even if I'm the disease. "Please, Rosie, there's got to be something. Tino said you were in summer school. What's going on?"

The last time I lashed out—at Mom, Dad, and Mr. Torrez—it didn't make me feel any better, and it made them all feel worse, so I want to save Miguel. “Miguel, you need to go,” I say.

“No, Rosie, not until you tell me why.” He tries to push his foot in the door. I stomp it.

“You need to go now,” I hiss. “If you try to get into this house or don’t leave, I’ll call the police, which is probably fine with you since you like men in uniform. Leave, now.”

“I don’t know what I can say that will make you less angry at me,” he says, but in my head I hear Dad’s voice saying the same thing. I should live in Echo Park.

“Miguel, leave.” He obeys without complaint this time. He’ll make a fine Marine. I wait until he’s at the curb before I throw his flowers and our future in the trash.

15

JUNE 11 / THURSDAY LATE EVENING

"Rosie, where are you going at this hour?" Mom asks as I head for the front door at eleven o'clock. "You have school tomorrow and there's a curfew. Get back into your room."

I use my new favorite word. "No."

"When I tell your father—"

"And where is he?" Dad's never here, which is fine. He's at the gym getting in shape or hanging with his vet friends, getting them to join him in another stint. Five to ten, like Alejandro.

"He's helping Victor," she says. I mimic someone drinking and then staggering. "If you must know, he's taking him to AA," Mom sighs. "Victor hasn't had a beer since he re-upped."

"Good for Victor," I snap. "Maybe I'll have one for him!"

"Rosie, you get back in!" is about all I hear before my feet hit the sidewalk in front of our house. I pull out my phone, see what the rest of the world is doing, and head out to nowhere.

* * *

"I'll need to see an ID," the SDPD white-skinned, blue-eyed young cop says. I got brown hands in my pocket, white hoodie on my head, black buds in my ears, but no ID I'll show him.

"How old are you?" he asks. I don't answer, but I know I look my age, maybe younger.

"Curfew is 10 p.m." I look at my phone. It's almost 1 a.m. There's a bunch of missed calls, texts, and messages. If only I cared about any of those people. "I'll take you home."

"I don't have a home."

"Fine, then we'll get you a placement in a shelter for tonight," he says. "Do your parents know where you are? Is there an adult that we can contact to let them know you're safe?"

"You ask a lot of questions; you must be stupid," are the last words I say before he slaps handcuffs on me. He takes my ID from my back pocket. "Rosalita Alvirde, you're under arrest."

16

JUNE 12 / FRIDAY MORNING

"Rosie, what are we going to do with you?" Mom says. The police guy lied—big surprise, a guy in a uniform breaking a promise to me—and didn't take me to juvie. Instead, he just brought me home. Mom and Dad's response was as predicted: yelling followed by shouting.

"What kind of example are you setting for Lucinda and Chavo?" Dad asks.

"What kind of example are you setting for Lucinda and Chavo?" I mock him.

"I am setting an example of a man doing what is best for his country and his family, even if ungrateful members of that family act like spoiled babies rather than mature young people."

I mock him now by bawling like a baby. "That's enough," Dad commands. I continue.

"Rosie, please stop it, you're upsetting—" I turn around. Lucinda and Chavo stand by the kitchen door, still in their pj's. "Lucinda, Chavo, please go back to your rooms," Mom says.

Dad rises from the table and paces like a caged tiger. He takes a deep breath and then walks toward me. He puts his arms on both sides of me; now I'm in the cage. "Rosalita Maria Alvirde, this is the last time we are having this conversation. I am sorry that my decision has angered you. Life doesn't always work out the way we have it planned. I am making the best decision I can. When I am a Marine, I matter. I mean something, not like how I am now."

He turns on his heels and walks toward the kitchen counter. He pours himself a cup of coffee like today was any other day. He wants things to go back to normal, which I realize for him means not being in this house, not being my dad. Defending Old Glory, not young Rosie.

"I want you to talk to Father Rodriquez," Mom says. Dad's got country, Mom's got God.

"You will go to school only," Dad says. "You will come right home. You will have no friends over. You will not leave this house without my permission. You will do this or else."

"Or else what?" I ask. Dad blows on his coffee, stares even hotter, and exits in silence.

17

JUNE 16 / TUESDAY AFTERNOON

“Rosie, wait up!” Brooke yells after me as I walk home from stupid summer school.

I slow down. I don’t really want to talk with her, but I’m going crazy being cut off from the world. When I got home from school yesterday, I found Dad had turned off my phone, ended the internet access from my computer, and put key locks on the doors leading outside. He had a tree service trim the oak by my bedroom. If I was getting out, I’d need to be a paratrooper.

"She's a terrible teacher, isn't she?" Brooke says in her "everyone but me is stupid" tone.

"Which one?" Unlike Brooke, who failed one course, I failed four, so my summer school day is full. She told me she sometimes hangs around summer school because she has no place to go.

"Mrs. Jackson," she answers. "Even that doofus Mr. Richards was better than her."

"You're right about that!" I let Brooke talk while I nod my head to pretend like I'm listening. I'm really thinking about Mr. Richards and how I let him down more than anyone.

"So, some of us are going to party tonight at Mission Beach. You in?" she asks.

"I've never been." When we go to the beach, it's as a family and on base at Pendleton.

"Really? It's a crazy scene, but I gotta steer clear of the west end," she says.

"Rival turf?" I assume if she's really gone white girl ghetto then she's jumped in a gang.

She laughs. "Nothing like that. That's where Tino hangs, and we're done. I caught him texting with some skank and now . . ." Brooke talks as fast and hard as a Santa Ana winds blows.

I cut her off. "I'm grounded." I tell her about breaking curfew: the icing on the crap cake. She laughs. I assume it's because she's high. Most kids at summer school seem to be.

"My dad said one more thing wrong and 'or else.'"

"Or else what?" she asks

I swallow hard. "I don't know yet if I want to find out."

18

JUNE 17 / WEDNESDAY MORNING

"Brooke Aaron?" Mrs. Jackson says. I bet I could say "here" and Jackson would never notice that indeed Brooke's seat is quite empty, but I've got no need for trouble with her.

"Rosie Alvirde?" I respond and she calls the rest of the roll. Unlike the Marine funerals during the wars when the lists got longer, summer school attendance get shorter with more kids dropping out. I fight the urge to join the deserters because all I need to do is get through the next two weeks.

Dad ships out for Parris Island on July 1. He'll be gone and life will be back to normal.

"This is the first assessment of the summer semester and . . ."

Just shut up and hand me the test, I think. When she does, I practically rip it out of her hands. I wait until she says "go" and then I rip through it, with answers I know are correct. I know this material, not because I memorized it or she said it, but because Mr. Richards taught it like a real teacher does. We've got some of those left, but most of them teach to the test, so you forget half the stuff.

I finish first. I've got time to kill before my next class, math, with the equally uninspiring Mr. Martin, so I head down to the commons since the library's not open in the summer. I find a table near the corner and pull out an old MP3 player I smuggled out of the house. I'm listening, without earbuds, to the greatest hits of my junior high years when a uniformed security officer comes over.

"You'll need to turn that down, or better yet, off," he says in an oh-not-so-friendly tone.

I point to the empty tables. "I'm not bothering anybody. Leave me alone."

"School policy is . . ." he's talking, but I'm not listening or watching his mouth. I'm just looking at the cheap fake gold buttons on his crummy blue uniform and that's close enough.

I stand, turn up the music, dance, and sing along with the "oorah" Marine chant. He tells me to sit, but I defy him. I keep dancing and oorahing until ten minutes later when more uniforms arrive. San Diego PD. And I know I got a blue uniform waiting for me at juvie. Oorah!

19

JUNE 18 / THURSDAY LATE AFTERNOON

"Did you learn anything?" Dad says as I walk out into the lobby. As I suspected, the school didn't press charges but my parents—Dad the decision maker, I'm sure—decided to let me spend almost two full days and a night at the Meadow Lark Drive Marriott, aka juvie hall.

"Yeah, I'm scared straight," I say, sounding as bored and unafraid as possible.

"The car's in the ramp," Dad says.

"Where's Mom?" He walks away, I stay in

place. He returns to me. As if.

"I didn't want her to see you here," Dad says. "Why are you breaking our hearts?"

Ever since Dad said he was re-enlisting, he's been asking me questions and expecting answers but I've only given him anger, silence, and defiance. And no apology for my behavior.

"I'm sorry." I finally say the words he wants to hear. Maybe it was the sleepless night on the thin mattress on the hard bed with the black girl on the right of me crying for her mother, the blond on the left threatening to kill the black girl if she didn't shut the f up, or me in the middle so scared that I almost forgot how to breathe at times. Maybe it's none of those things.

"Rosie, you can't keep on like this. It's killing your mother."

I nod in silence.

"If you keep messing up, you'll spend more than one night here. Understand?"

"Yes." I think about Miguel's brother doing ten years and I can't imagine it. From the other inmates—they called us residents, like it was a Marriott—acting all kinds of stupid, to the correctional officers acting all kinds of tough, I never want to spend another second there.

"If Father's Day wasn't Sunday, I would've left you in there longer, but since it is the last Father's Day before I ship out—"

I cut him off there. I want to hug him, but I can't. I don't say what I'm really afraid of—*it might be the last Father's Day before you die.*

20

JUNE 21 / SUNDAY EARLY EVENING
FATHER'S DAY

"Who brought the beer?" I ask Mom as I point at the six, down to two, pack of Tecate. "You know Victor and Dad aren't drinking since they're getting ready for . . ."

"Me." Mom takes the cozy off the can. I'd thought she'd been drinking soda. "I don't know if I can make it through this day without it."

She motions for me to sit next to her at the

table, where she's wrapping leftovers. The rest of the family, including Grandma Rita, is outside on a perfect San Diego summer evening.

She starts to talk but takes another sip of beer, then a large swallow. I've never seen her like this, but from Victor, I've sure seen what drunk looks like. "Mom, can I ask something?"

Another swallow I guess means yes.

"A few weeks ago, Dad said you threatened to leave him if he re-enlisted. Is that true?"

Another swallow.

"But it was a bluff, right?"

Swallow.

"Is that how you got him home in the first place?" I ask.

She sets the beer on the table, and I grab before she can pick it up again. I don't need torture to get the truth, just Tecate.

"Yes, Rosie, yes, and I was wrong but I couldn't do it anymore," she says, words only slightly slurred. "You were getting older, Lucinda, Chavo, working two jobs. It was too much."

"Then why is he going back?" I ask. "I bet it was Victor's idea since he's got nothing."

"Have you asked your father?" she asks me. "All I've seen you do since he told you is slam doors, yell, run away, and behave like a wild child. You're almost an adult. Act like one."

* * *

I find Dad outside with Victor and some other Marine buddies who must not have kids or dads to celebrate Father's Day. There's lots of laughing, and I know it's something I can't really understand. I have friends at school, although I stopped hanging around with them as much when Miguel came along, but I can tell it's not the same. That's friendship; this is kinship.

"Dad?" I yell out. He waves, smiles, and motions for me to join him. I shake my head and stand my ground. He whispers something to Victor and walks toward me. Behind him, Lucinda's taking pictures with a camera. She's artistic; I'm scientific. We make a good team.

Chavo and Grandma Rita seemed to have disappeared. "Dad, can I ask you something?"

"What is it, Rosie?" We lean against the back porch. The wood stiffens my back.

I take a deep breath, steady myself, and say it. "Why? Why are you doing this?"

As I wait for his answer, I don't cry or act emotional. I'll be an adult; he'll respect that.

He puts his hand on my shoulder. "Rosie, it's not just one reason, so it's hard to . . ."

"I want to know." I put my hand over the one resting on my shoulder. "I need to know."

"I'm tired of fighting with the VA, your mother, and these know-nothing managers in these terrible jobs," Dad barks. "They say I'm a hero, yet I can't get or keep a good job. If I go back in the Corps and serve some more years, then I can retire early. Enjoy my family."

"But what if?"

The hand presses harder. "I made it through two wars. There won't be another. America doesn't have the stomach for it. Rosie, it's the only thing I'm good at. I'm a soldier. I told you stories of how I was back in the day, getting in trouble, acting all kinds of stupid. I was headed nowhere. We were broke, then Lucinda came along. I was out of choices, so I joined the Corps. It helped me become the man I needed to be."

"I want you here." I lose it. Dad pulls me tight; he's my tear sponge. "I'll miss you."

He whispers kind words in Spanish but says nothing else. Behind us, we hear a commotion. We turn and there's Chavo and Grandma Rita. She's dressed him up in a pretend Marine uniform. She pushes him toward Dad.

"Like father, like son!" Dad says.

I don't see Chavo the boy, I think of Chavo in twenty years: the man, the father, the fallen hero. As Dad reaches out to embrace his youngest, his oldest walks away, head down, creating a path of tears.

"Rosie, wait up!" Dad yells after me. I speed ahead, double time, but he catches up with me on the sidewalk thanks to his crash fitness program. "You can't run away from this."

I wipe my nose and turn off the tears. "Why not—you're running away from us again!"

He motions for me to come closer, but I cross my arms across my chest.

"I told you—"

"I don't believe you," I snap, feeling stupid for getting suckered in by his false reasons. "If you loved us you would—"

"It is complicated." He kicks his right foot against the pavement beneath us.

"No, Daddy, it is real simple." My arms leave my chest; my fingers bawl into fists and I start bouncing punches off Dad's chest. "It's like you want to die."

"How can you say that? You're not making any sense!"

Another punch, left, then right. "But, Chavo, do you have to doom him as well?"

He catches my flying fists in his big paws. "Rosie, grow up."

I wrestle free from his grasp. "I will!" I shout and run away again, but this time he doesn't chase me. I don't believe him or trust him; *always faithful* is the opposite of what he is to me. If he wants me to grow up, I know just the place to do that: Mission Beach.

21

JUNE 21 / SUNDAY LATE EVENING
FATHER'S DAY

"Does this bus go to Mission Beach?" I ask the driver. Downtown San Diego's spooky at night, mostly deserted except around the bus transfer mall. He motions me onboard. About now I bet Dad's wishing he hadn't taken away my cell phone. I wonder how long it took everyone else to notice I had left the party.

Since I left in a hurry, I have nothing but the clothes on my back. They're party pretty, unlike the ugliness of Chavo's mock Marine uniform. What was Grandma Rita thinking?

The bus goes through neighborhoods I've never seen before and I realize how small my world really is and how I've made it smaller. Cut off from my old friends because of Miguel, cut off from Miguel because of me, I'm as alone as a person could be. At home, Mom's obviously surrendered to Dad's wishes, while Lucinda's now acting like the obedient second child.

The scene at Mission Beach is, as Brooke described, crazy even on a Sunday night. The bus drops me near the center entrance where a homeless horde acts as a welcoming committee. I take off my shoes and feel sand run through my toes. The sands here are almost gold; the sands of Iraq and Afghanistan are still stained with blood from the past and maybe will be again.

I walk with my head up, soaking it all in. There's people drinking, people playing beach volleyball, and more people drinking. I take in the sunset and start looking for a place to sleep.

"Hey, Rosie Alvirde!" I hear a voice call from ten feet in front of me. I squint and the shape begins to take form. It's Tino Estrada, Miguel's cousin and Brooke's ex. I wave.

He runs toward me. He's got a long white shirt unbuttoned and jeans rolled up at the ankles. When he gets closer, I notice he's got green eyes, the same color as the tattoos on his broad chest. The one on his arm—the tag of the NCA, National City Amigos—is mostly red.

"What are you doing down here?" he asks. "This is the wrong place for someone—"

And like taking a test, I immediately know the right answer. "Looking for you."

22

JUNE 22 / MONDAY LATE MORNING

"You awake?" Tino whispers into my ear.

We burned and crashed: burned our fingertips on many a blunt and then crashed on the beach. Tino's next to me, shirtless. I mumble: my mouth as dry as the ocean is wet.

"Be right back," he mumbles and then kisses me on the top of the head. When he walks away, I see that his back—like his arms, front, and legs—is a canvas of ink and stories.

But what's my story? I don't remember

anything after we switched from beer to tequila. I'm not shirtless, my bra's still on, and my jeans still snapped. My body doesn't feel any different. Honor? Respect? Tino?

I feel dizzy, thinking about what could have happened. I push the feeling away. I can take care of myself—I'm good at figuring out who to trust.

When Tino comes back a few minutes later, he's got a cigarette dangling from his mouth. He fires it up with a skull and bones lighter. When he gets closer, he offers me a drag.

"No, thanks," I say casually, like it's something I do every day. "What time is it?"

He laughs, takes a drag, but doesn't pull out his phone. "You got some place to go?"

I think about home, school, Dad. "No."

He sits down on the sand next to me. While my clothes are still on, they're not clean. I feel sand everywhere, especially between my toes. "School. Crap jobs. Curfews. I'm past it."

I start to rise, but he pulls me back against him. It feels comforting in a way. He smells of smoke, weed, and sweat. I start to ask him about last night, but I know we did something, I'm just hoping nothing I regret. He's got his right arm across my chest.

"Where'd you get it?" I ask as I move his arm away from me, hold it a few inches in front, and point to the NCA tat.

He says nothing, only puts his arms back where it was, but tighter.

"I want one," I say, not sure why.

Tino inhales and blows the smoke down my neck. "You don't just get one," he says in a tone that makes me feel so stupid. "You gotta earn it. You gotta jump in. Join Up. Family Forever."

Semper Fi. *Familia para siempre.* Men plus mottoes give life meaning and purpose.

23

JUNE 25 / THURSDAY EVENING

"Lucinda, listen. It's Rosie," I say into the prepaid cell that Tino bought me.

"Where are you?" she shouts.

"Listen, I called to tell you that I'm okay."

"We're going crazy with worry. They have the police looking for you. And . . ."

She goes on but I tune her out. I don't want to hear how I'm breaking their hearts, how worried everybody is, and all of that. I wait for her to say the words, but she doesn't.

"So, is Dad still shipping out on July 1?" I ask.

"He's got his orders."

"So, like if I was dead, do you think he'd still go?"

Lucinda starts to cry. "Don't you ever say anything like that again! I'm telling Mom . . ."

"I don't want to talk to them," I hiss. "I'll see them real soon."

I look down on my virgin arm. I couldn't do that. I look down on the rest of my virgin self and know that Tino's not taking no for an answer much longer. Feeling his arms around me is a good distraction, but if I'm hanging on the beach with him, there's a high price to pay.

"Rosie, I have to . . ." is as far as she gets before I hang up the phone.

"Hey, let's go," Tino says as he pats me on the butt of the jeans he bought for me. Well, he said he bought them, but since my role was to distract the clerk, I know what's what.

"What's going on?"

He seems in a hurry.

"I got a call from my man Freddie. He needs me down at Mission Beach ASAP."

"Is there a . . . fight or something?" I ask. I can't think of the right word for gang war.

"He said he needs my help." He's walking in front of me. "Bunch of Marines there."

"Tino, you don't want to fight with Marines." Dad punching out Tino comes to mind.

He laughs. "Fight? He needs help moving product. Those jarheads are great customers."

24

JUNE 26 / FRIDAY LATE AFTERNOON

"Your parents are outside," the burly white CO says. He motions for me to stand. I've already changed out of the stuff they made me wear when they kept me in a holding cell.

I got myself arrested, more or less on purpose, since I'm out of other ideas. I went back to the same store I'd been in with Tino and got popped for shoplifting. It seemed like something bad enough to get me hauled in here, but not so bad that it would cause me real problems. I bet there are more girls at school who boost their clothes than buy them. I never thought I'd be one, but then again, I never thought my dad would re-enlist in the Marines and leave me again.

The loud clank of the door startles me, but more surprising is that it's Mom there to pick me up, not Dad. She's crying like somebody died. "Rosalita, Rosalita," she keeps saying.

"I'm sorry, Mom." She offers a hug and I take it. It's only a thousand times better than Tino having his hands on me. "I'm sorry I'm putting you and Daddy through all this."

"Dad talked to the store. They won't be pressing charges, so you—"

I break away. "Why would he do that?"

"He's trying to protect you, Rosie." She says it like I should know.

"Then why isn't he staying home!" A skinny white woman in the waiting room gives me a dirty look. "Then why is he leaving us again?"

She pulls me back toward her. I don't resist.

"Rosie, he told you all that. I don't want him to go either, but he's decided it's what's best for him and he thinks it's best for us, too."

"You tell him that if he goes, I'm going to join him."

"What are you talking about, Rosie? You're too—"

"I'll do something worse than shoplift. I'll get a blue uniform, I'll get to stand in line, follow orders, and risk getting killed. If he goes back into the Marines," I say, pointing at the door, "I go back in there."

25

JUNE 28 / SUNDAY EARLY MORNING

"It's time," Mom says as I emerge from my room. It has to be her, since Dad's still not talking to me. His yelling is bad; his silent treatment is worse. He's got two more days at home.

I'm all dressed in churchgoing clothes, just like I'll be dressed again for school. All that acting out got me nothing; all it did was cause me to lose respect, for myself and from my family.

"You look nice, Rosie," Lucinda says. She's shining like the sun. She got her room back on

Friday. Victor decided to spend his last few days with another family: the Tecates, I guess.

The ride to church is funeral silent between me and Dad. Everybody else is talking like it's just another day. Don't they know that the next time we're with Dad in church, he won't sit in the pew with us because he'll be in a casket in the front? Marines die; it's what they do.

I sit through the endless rituals of church, where people say amen rather than oorah, but it's all the same. Somebody far away is calling the shots and everybody else is supposed to follow. I take communion as my opportunity. I go last in my family but keep walking past the pew. Not wanting to create a scene, or maybe they just are tired of me, nobody chases after me.

The blessed-are-the-poor homeless act like human shields when I arrive on the bus to Mission Beach. There are fewer of them than I've seen in the past: these must be the hardcore cases. No shelters, no swapping prayers for food. First in, last out. The Marines of street people.

"Change?" A shirtless bum with one leg says. I move past him on my way west. Tino's my last shot to change Dad's mind. Six weeks ago Tino's ROTC cousin trembled as he kissed me on prom night. The world changes in six weeks, six days, six minutes, six seconds. I feel a tap on my back. The homeless guy. "You got nothing for me after I gave myself for you?"

I turn. I don't want to stare at where his leg used to be. "I don't have any . . ." I start to say but stop when I notice not his missing leg, but the tattoo on his right arm: Semper Fi.

I turn around and head back toward the bus. "What you are running from?" the guy shouts after me. "Must be nice! I can't run any more."

I don't respond because I don't have a good answer. I'm not running away, I want to tell him, I'm running in circles, faster and faster, getting dizzier and dizzier, except seeing him missing a leg was like a kick in the head. I see stars, and stripes, as I jump on the first bus that stops. The bus to go home. Nothing is going to bring that guy's leg back, nothing's going to change Dad's mind. Always means forever, and how can I change forever?

26

JUNE 29 / MONDAY MORNING

"I told Miguel about you hooking up with Tino," is Brooke's greeting to me on my return to summer school.

"I'm not hooking up—" I begin.

"I heard Miguel cried like a baby when Tino told him," Brooke says.

"It's not like that." I take my seat, sadly next to Brooke. Mrs. Jackson clears her throat, trying to get people's attention, but it's not working. Classroom chaos.

Brooke laughs, way too loud. "Been there, done him, so don't tell me that."

"Brooke Aaron?" Mrs. Jackson says. Brooke ignores her, focuses on me.

"He's gonna cheat on you like he did with me," she hisses. Her eyes narrow to slits.

"Rosalita Alvirde?" Mrs. Jackson calls. I give her a grunt response. She doesn't welcome me back or acknowledge I went AWOL. Nobody missed me. I'm used to it.

"Matter of fact, it makes me think that maybe you were the skank he was—"

"Brooke, shut up."

Her right arm reaches across the valley between our desks. "Make me, skank." I push back in my chair. It screeches. Mrs. Jackson's reaction is to call the next name and the next.

"Brooke, I don't want any trouble. I—"

"Too bad, Rosie, because I do!" She's on me in seconds, pulling my hair with her left hand and throwing punches with her right. I defend myself, trying to scratch her accusing eyes.

The already chaotic classroom explodes into a riot of cheers and jeers. Brooke knocks me to the floor and she's on top of me like some wild animal. "Nobody takes what's mine!"

I want to punch the Marine Corps for the same reason, but since they're not available, I aim for Brooke's always stuck-up nose. *Crack.* My knuckle. Her nose. Maybe both.

27

JUNE 29 / MONDAY AFTERNOON

"It was self-defense," I told the school security officer. Since he's the one I had a problem with earlier, I knew he didn't believe me. He thinks I'm just all bad attitude.

"Doesn't matter, fighting is fighting," Mr. Blue Shirt in a black and white world said. They took me to the nurse's office and bandaged my hand, but they took Brooke to the hospital. After that, I got escorted to the office of the summer school principal, Mrs. Logan, but she didn't say a word, just told me to wait. And that's what I've been doing for about three hours. Waiting.

"Come with me," Mrs. Logan said as she emerged from her office. During the school year she teaches drama. Teaching drama to high schoolers: the most needless job in the world.

I do as I'm told, something I used to be good at, and follow her from her office. She says nothing, so maybe like Dad, she thinks the silent treatment is punishment enough. We take a short walk into the counseling suite, which is odd because counselors take the summer off.

"She's here," Mrs. Logan says as she opens the door. There, dressed for summer, not for school, are both Mr. Torrez and Mr. Richards. She drops me, I hope, not behind enemy lines.

Mr. Torrez motions for me to sit at the table with the two of them. The grim looks on their faces clue me that somebody's told them about summer school troublemaker Rosalita Alvirde. They look at each other—the slouchy science teacher and the former Marine turned school counselor—like two members of the firing squad wondering which of them fires the kill shot.

Finally, it's Mr. Richards. "Why?" Three letters. One word. World of hurt.

I tell them, since nobody else wants to know. Mom and Dad listen, but they don't hear.

They don't say much. Richards asks a question every now and then, while Torrez keeps nodding, repeating what I say, and if he's not actually concerned, he's Oscar material. I manage to tell them just about everything, except details about Tino, until I can't talk through the tears.

28

JUNE 29 / MONDAY LATE AFTERNOON

"You seen Tino?" I ask Freddie, one of Tino's west end crew. He shrugs.

As I walk Mission Beach, the words of Mr. Torrez and Mr. Richards ring in my head, or rather the lack of words. They didn't tell me what to do, as I talked. They let me recount how stupid I'd been. They let me say for myself that the smart thing to do was be like a Marine: always faithful to my best self.

I'm torn about Tino. Part of me wants to

thank him for protecting me—my time as a runaway could have been much worse. But part of me wants to slap him for taking advantage of me when I was vulnerable, pressuring me for sex when all I wanted was a friend. When I find him, my heart will tell me which part wins.

I'm not as torn about Brooke, but I should apologize even though she started it. It was making me fight for my honor that set the wheels in motion for me to wake up finally and fly right.

I know now I'm not changing Dad's mind, so I'm just hurting myself. Dad is leaving no matter what, so I might as well make things right before he leaves. And I'm hurting Mom, too, at a time when she needs me. I know she feels like I do about Dad leaving.

But I still feel a rock in my stomach when I think about all that Dad's already missed and all he'll miss when he's gone again. And I still can't push away the fear that he'll miss out on everything permanently. Will he be here when I get married? When I have kids? To see Chavo graduate?

But do we want an angry drunk dad for all those things? Why does it have to be a choice between depression or risking death?

After making a circle around the west end, I tell Freddie I'll catch up with Tino later. I'm on my way back to the bus stop and home for dinner, one of my last with Dad, when I see him.

Not Tino, but the one-legged homeless Marine. He asks for money. I empty my pockets. "Thanks," he mumbles through a mouth hidden under a jungle of dirty facial hair.

"What happened?" I ask, keeping my distance.

He looks at the space that used to be occupied by a leg. "I was in Fallujah," he begins. He's pretty messed up so he repeats lots of the story, but I get the gist. It's like the stories I've heard Victor and Dad tell many times. Wrong place. Wrong time. I'd add wrong war.

"Then what?"

He starts to tell the story again from the

beginning, but that's not what I need to know.

"No, I meant what happened after. Why are you here? I know the VA has—"

His response is mostly four letter words, cursing the VA, the government, but mostly the Marines for letting him down. "Always faithful, my ass. Worst decision I ever made."

"Joining the Marines?"

"No, leaving. There I was somebody. Here, I'm nothing."

29

JULY 1 / WEDNESDAY MORNING

"Double time, Rosie," Dad yells over the noise of the alarm on my phone. I've been dressed for hours since I never really slept last night, haunted by the fear of nightmares about Dad dying if I closed my eyes.

"I'm ready," I shout back. If I shout the lie, does that mean it is true?

The knob turns easily since Dad removed the lock. He walks into my room slowly, without a word. He shuts the door behind him and pulls up a chair next to my bed. I sit up.

"You look nice," Dad says.

"So do you." He's in the blue dress uniform for the flight to South Carolina. Since I rejoined my family, I've learned some of the details about how long he'll be back in basic (six weeks) and where he'll head after that (back to San Diego) until he's deployed, most likely—because of his experience—to a unit overseas.

"I'm sorry about everything," I tell him for the hundredth time it seems, certainly a hundred more times this summer than I'd ever said it before in my life. "Things just got out of control."

He puts his hand on my shoulder. Even though he's strong, the hand lies softly. "Rosie, I should've talked this over with all of you before announcing my decision, so I'm to blame as well. But I know where I need to be. I know who I am. I'm not a Home Depot manager, I'm not a McDonald's shift leader, and I'm not even a stay-at-home dad. I'm a warrior. I fight to defend my country. I'm a Marine always."

"And always faithful."

"I know you won't believe this," he says, which means he expects me to. "But I'm doing this for you, for Lucinda, and especially for Chavo. I'd rather have you growing up without me here, but knowing I did something more important than hanging around until I become a person I don't want to be. Until I turn into Victor or somebody like that. You understand?"

I think about the homeless guy on the beach. Did he have a family?

"Yeah, actually, I do."

30

JULY 4 / SATURDAY LATE MORNING

"I can't see!" Chavo shouts. Lucinda and I hoist him up for a moment as another high school ROTC unit marches by. I've yet to see the one from my school; I've yet to see Miguel.

"Do you remember that parade where it rained?" Lucinda asked. "Dad was in it."

"I remember them all," I say, almost having to shout over the noise from the crowd and the marching bands. The ones I remember most are the ones where Dad was home.

Chavo's heavy and I let him slide to the ground to rest my arms.

"I still can't see!" Chavo shouts. Too bad because he's missing quite the show, but he's got plenty of them in his future. If Dad gets what he wants, Chavo will march in one himself.

"Let me have him," Mom says. She takes him from us and puts him on her shoulders. Mom's not much taller, but she sure is stronger. She's had to be, and I guess it's my turn now. Those were the last words Dad said just before he headed for his flight. "Rosalita, stay strong."

I didn't have time to ask him what he meant by that, but I got a pretty good idea. Go to school. Study. Stop acting out. Be a good sister. Be a good daughter. In short, be who I was before.

"Is that your school's unit?" Lucinda points toward the parade.

I step forward and see the familiar banner. Behind the flag bearers come the officers. Miguel and the other captains lead the other cadets as they march one two oorah down the street.

"Miguel!" I call out. He doesn't acknowledge me, or maybe he didn't hear me. "Miguel!" I call again, but he's focused on his leadership role, like I should be.

The parade continues, but I've lost interest, like I assume Miguel's lost interest in me. We stay for another hour until Crown Prince Chavo's whining hits a fever pitch that even Mom can't tolerate, so she tells us we're leaving. And Dad said he'd try to Facetime with us this afternoon. Lucinda and I breathe a sigh of relief.

But my relief turns to caution when I see Freddie and Tino standing near the corner, laughing at something. I crane my neck. It's the two of them and a guy with one leg.

"Meet you at the car," I tell my family.

31

JULY 4 / SATURDAY EARLY AFTERNOON

"Look who's here, *ese*," Tino cracks to Freddie when they see me. They pull the homeless guy with them into an alley.

"What are you doing here?" I ask Tino, following. Freddie, as always, just shrugs. About the only time he talks is when he's making a sale. Tino doesn't answer me either. He owes me nothing. I get it.

"You okay?" I ask the homeless guy. He slides down against the wall of the alley, landing on a ground covered with garbage. Good citizens crowd the sidewalk today so the back alleys belong to the Tino types.

"He's fine, or about to be." Tino hands the guy a packet of white powder. In return, the homeless guy hands Tino not loose change but a crisp bill.

Something kicks in. "You don't need that," I tell the guy. "Stay strong."

This cracks Tino and Freddie. "He's strong. He's a Marine," Tino says. "So you think this is how your old man is going to end up, Rosie? High as a kite yet still on the ground."

I reach for the packet, but the vet buries it in the pocket of his torn jeans.

"Stay out of my business," Tino says. "You had a chance. You just needed to—"

"I don't need anything from you, Tino."

"That's right, you got it all," Tino says and then starts mocking me, telling Freddie and the vet all the stuff I told him when I was high. I don't remember saying most of it, although they were things I felt when I was at my lowest. "All those Marine guys are so stupid."

"Shut up, Tino," I hiss.

"I mean marching off to some war, getting killed for no reason, just—"

"What do you think the NCA is? How is that different?"

Tino stares at me. "We die for family, not for country. Family Forever!"

I stare back at Tino. His look is so hard for someone so young. The vet looks older than his years as well. Wars on the streets and overseas age a person too fast. Like them, like me.

32

JULY 6 / MONDAY MORNING

"You wanted to see me, Mrs. Logan?" I ask as I walk into the office after first period.

She motions for me to sit. I obey. "I've spoken with the security officers, your teacher, and some other students. It does seem you were attacked and defending yourself, but still there are consequences. After speaking with Mr. Richards and Mr. Torrez, we've decided that your behavior doesn't seem conducive to a classroom setting, so you'll finish summer school in this office. Each morning bring your books and you'll do all your assignments and tests. You've missed so much of the term, this is the only way you'll get caught up and not fall further behind."

"Thank you," I whisper.

"Your father is in the Corps, right?" I nod. The fact she asked tells me that Mr. Richards and Mr. Torrez got her to agree with this without giving her the whole story. They protected me.

"Well, consider this to be like basic training. In the next three weeks, you'll work as hard as you've ever worked. If you do the work, then you'll be able to start your senior year in the fall."

"I want that very much."

"I also suggest for those subjects in which you're struggling, you find a tutor," she says. She reaches onto her desk and hands me a sheet of paper with a list of names and numbers. They're in alphabetical order by first name so Miguel's name is right in the middle. "One last thing."

I nod as I pretend to record Miguel's number even though it's tattooed on my brain.

"Mr. Richards suggested that you look into some of the VA teen programs or investigate groups on the base that help young people through the deployment of a parent. How about that?"

"I've gone to them before," I confess. "I didn't really think they helped."

"Mr. Richards said he thought you could train to facilitate. He believes you're a leader."

"That's a lot to do. I'd better hurry up," I say. "I'd better do double time."

ABOUT THE AUTHOR

Patrick Jones is the author of more than twenty novels for teens. He has also written two nonfiction books about combat sports, *The Main Event*, on professional wrestling, and *Ultimate Fighting*, on mixed martial arts. He has spoken to students at more than one hundred alternative schools, including residents of juvenile correctional facilities. Find him on the web at www.connectingya.com and on Twitter: @PatrickJonesYA.

SUPPORT
AND
DEFEND

SUPPORT
AND
DEFEND
ALWAYS
FAITHFUL
PATRICK JONES

SUPPORT
AND
DEFEND
COLLATERAL
DAMAGE
PATRICK JONES / BRENT CHARTIER

SUPPORT
AND
DEFEND
COMBAT
ZONE
PATRICK JONES

SUPPORT
AND
DEFEND
FREEDOM
FLIGHT
PATRICK JONES